Early Praise for
MIDWEST FUTURES

"The flyover zone has never been so fruitful! The stories and poems in *Midwest Futures* will rattle your bones and imaginations. Better yet, you off-planet recruiters will find plenty of new candidates in these pages. These writers are folks who know the land and can tap its full potential. The generations here are close to the old ways. They still know the secrets—the dangers and banalities—of water, wind, and sun—the lore of transforming alien landscapes. Highly recommended!"

—Dennis Maulsby, author of the novel *House de Gracie*,
and collections including *The Fantasy Works* and *Free Fire Zone*

"A body cannot go on living once the heart ceases its circulation of blood—likewise, the country and our bordering and distant neighbors need the pulse of the Heartland. Like Joni Mitchell, who sang, 'You don't know what you've got 'til it's gone,' the poems and prose of *Midwest Futures* are glimpses into what might happen if more eco-friendly ways are not embraced. The losses of natural beauty and food on our plates and clear waters need not be; "[a] time [can] occur / when you can walk again / and breathe again / with no fire hazing / the horizon."

—Lisa Stice, author of multiple poetry collections,
including *Letters from Conflict*, *Permanent Change of Station*,
and the forthcoming *From Reluctant Earth*

"The sense of wonder established by the cover illustration of *Midwest Futures* is fulfilled time and again with the poems and brief stories on the inside. Yes, there are cosmic queens, colonies on Mars, and scenes of nature fighting back against humans. But it's the many different imaginings of a future that somehow, some way, will always be there that makes this collection so surprisingly comforting to read."
—Bill McCloud, author of the poetry collections
The Error of the Stars
and *The Smell of the Light: Vietnam, 1968-1969*

"The poems gently place the reader in the waving Midwest fields, then blast off, rockets and church spires piercing the grey sky. Looking into the future as much as at the ground beneath our feet, these poems reflect and resonate."
—Aly Allen, author of the poetry collection
Paying for Gas with Quarters:
a Parent's Odyssey in Poems

Midwest Futures

Poems & Micro-Stories
from Tomorrow's Heartland

Edited by Randy Brown
Middle West Press LLC
Johnston, Iowa

Anthology / Science-Fiction Flash & Poetry

ISBN (print): 978-1-953665-32-4
ISBN (e-book): 978-1-953665-33-1
Library of Congress Control Number: 2024949666

Middle West Press LLC
P.O. Box 1153
Johnston, Iowa 50131-9420
www.middlewestpress.com

Special thanks to Aiming Circle patrons
Nathan Didier of Cedar Falls, Iowa
Tim Lynch of McAllen, Texas

"Write what you know; write where you are."

CONTENTS

Discussion & Writing Prompts

Foreword

When people think about pop-culture references to the Midwest, they're usually looking back to the past. Middle Westerners, after all, have got the nostalgia-vibes market locked down tight.

In literature, we've got "The Music Man" and "State Fair" and "The Wizard of Oz." We've got "Our Town," "A Thousand Acres," and "The Bridges of Madison County." We've got Willa Cather, Sinclair Lewis, and F. Scott Fitzgerald. All good stuff, but doesn't it all seem so ... last-century?

Yes, Captain Kirk's birthplace is canonically Riverside, Iowa. Technically, however, that blessed event won't happen until the year 2233. In the meantime, what else do we have to look forward to?

The contributors to this anthology cultivated new visions and interpretations of the American Midwest's character, population, and landscape. By winnowing the chaff of old geographic and cultural stereotypes, they achieved a bumper crop of fresh narrative prospects!

Some of their visions are dark and brooding. Others are chock-full of gee-whiz positivity. Each item is rich with possibility, and Midwestern grit.

To inspire and motivate further explorations, on page 69, you can find a special bonus section of 7 discussion-starters and prompts, for use in workshops, book clubs, classrooms, and other gatherings. Each prompt is based on a selection of stories and poems found in the anthology!

Thanks for reading, dreaming, and creating! *"See you in the future!"*

—*Randy "Sherpa" Brown*

Poems & Micro-Stories

Rain Country
by Bella Rotker

We raise cattle to be slaughtered
    under the wide green sky. Spare nothing.
        The clouds are always thick like dark feathers,

a fresh cut of beef on the table
    next to a serving bowl of potatoes. My
        mother passes around clippings from the herald.

Birth announcements, obituaries. Like any
    girl, I am learning to become
        between betweens and all these hills

rolling like knots of clay rising from under
    the grass. The plumes of smoke. The open
        mouth of a goat on the prairie. Apricots fall

in slow motion. I sink my teeth into one
    and consider my girlhood: a snake writhes
        in front of me, body pink and raw where its head

has come off. I sit in front of it and know
    it will die. I carve a hole in the warm earth
        next to the tree and fill it with blossoms.

Like most things, I know I should feel bad for it,
    the careful end of one's life spent observed,
        but I don't. I carry it to the grave and whisper

a prayer as a siren blares in the distance.
    There's nothing really to do around here
        but pray and I am glad to have something

to pray for. I wipe its blood on the shirt Mother washed
    in the river yesterday. I can see my breath
        as the fog settles in. Clouds

twisting into funnels against dark sunsets. Cattle
    running for the hills. It's not beautiful but I wish
        it was. Between betweens there's me

and the apricots. A girl becoming.
    I hum hymns until my father calls me
        inside to hide in the basement

with my brothers. When this passes, we will praise
    God, chase the animals back
        into their pastures. I am a servant

to this world of hurt. Always something
    undoing. Cicadas singing in the dark
        of night. In the morning, we will rise

and return to our work. There are hides
    to stretch and clean. Linens to rewash.

Bella Rotker is a proud Venezuelan and 305 local. A 5-time YoungArts winner and Best of The Net nominee, her work appears in Fifth Wheel Press, JAKE, Best American High School Writing *(2022 & 2023), and others. When she's not writing or making shadow puppets, Rotker is thinking about cafecitos and bodies of water. The poem "Rain Country" was previously recognized as a YoungArts winner in spoken word. Visit: bit.ly/bellarotker*

So Long, Lake of Stars
by Martin Ott

From my bedroom window, Lake Huron
danced in another dimension as I read
sci-fi and surfed toward distant shores.
My Converse glided atop glassy chop,
the monsters below pulsing quasar light.
Only Atlantean ships could transport me
from gym class. The waves I wrestled
were weapons from mutant warlords,
destructive beams I beat into submission.
My heroism nearly outpaced my imagination.
Space sirens held no sway, their echoes
trapped in the ice of my pubescent veins.
The blue eye of a cosmic queen watched
me leave this incandescent universe behind
on the fateful day I joined the Army. I sailed
into unknown lands, far ahead of my future.

Martin Ott is the author of twelve books of poetry and fiction, including a forthcoming book of prose poetry, Sharks vs. Selfies *(Black Spring Press Group). His first two poetry collections won the De Novo and Sandeen Prizes. His work has appeared in more than 300 magazines and 20 anthologies. A former U.S. Army interrogator and longtime Los Angeles resident, Ott develops for TV and film in-between other writing projects.*

statue on the nightstand
by Haley Vallejo

a statue of la virgen de guadalupe rests on the nightstand,
the rays of sun behind her are gilded in chipped, cheap gold,
gold like the kernels of corn that the hands of dying fathers, brothers,
mothers and sisters pull from the ground, in the hopes of a new start,
of a new life. neither will come, but hope is all that could fit
in a backpack, pressed against your side, cramped in the corner
of a trailer traveling from monterrey, mexico to anywhere, usa.

in the back of a trailer, still as a statue. like the statue of la virgen,
who looks at you with kindness, and it feels like mocking,
because she doesn't bring you fresh roses even though you have worked
so hard for them. you have worked so hard. and all you have
    to show for it
is a path of marigolds leading to dead fathers, brothers,
    mothers and sisters
who lay in the ground that sprouts gold corn. or was it cucumbers?
maybe it was blueberries. maybe it doesn't matter.

maría and jesús linger by the ofrenda, but they're not mary and jesus;
maría did not die untouched and jesús never resurrected.
they are your cousins, twice removed, who always came home
with nothing but bruises, and when you stare into paper eyes
painted on prayer cards or carved into statues, offering something
just out of reach, you think, *yo prefiero maría y jesús*, at least they
were honest when they said they were dying.

their bodies are still beneath the dirt, lungs swollen from dust
and chemicals and the fear of exile jumbled with the fear
of never leaving, of never getting paid to stay even when the air
killed their friends like flies, as if the real targets were cracked hands

and hungry stomachs. you are the only one left. the house is filled
with you and a family of ghosts, of maría and jesús' footsteps
creaking on the floorboards, crushing the termites into a paste.

like la virgen, they, too, are haloed by light, but the golden rays
are not gilded; the warmth fills the house, but you are sick of the sun,
sick of the blisters, sick of waiting for roses when all that grows
is marigolds, sick of being forced to pick fruit instead of flowers
until your fingers bleed. one day, you will join maría and jesús,
you will follow the marigolds, all the way back to monterrey,
in the back of a trailer speeding down the bumpy roads to heaven.

la virgen will greet you on the nightstand.

*Haley Vallejo is a writer from San Antonio, Texas and is now located in
Waco. As a recent graduate from Baylor University, she has undergraduate
degree in English literature and philosophy. When she isn't writing, she
likes to play with her pet cat and watch Formula 1. This poem first appeared
in* The Phoenix Literary Magazine.

Man of Tomorrow
by Eric Esquivel

I love the idea of Midwestern values being the driving force behind "The Man Of Tomorrow"—a "strange visitor from another planet" landing in the lap of a couple of midwestern corn farmers, and having "The American Way" engrained into their upbringing.

I grew up on the outskirts of Chicago, but my mom is from Nashua, Iowa, pop. 1,500. She never let go of that small-town way of moving through life:

Taking two hours to get the mail because she had to stop and talk to every neighbor she encountered on the way and ask—with genuine interest—about their lives. And the lives of their children. And their grandchildren. And their pets.

Having a vague knowledge of world affairs, but being absolutely-up-to-the-minute on any and all gossip pertaining to my apartment complex. Including the marital status of our mailman.

Knowing how much everyone is paying for rent. And who is going through a hard time, and might benefit from a neighborly invite to Sunday dinner.

Scoffing at things like jewelry, tattoos, and expensive shoes because they're "showy" and "prideful" ... but spending hundreds of dollars on Christmas, Halloween—and even Saint Patrick's Day—for the enjoyment of the neighborhood kids.

How could any being, "super" or otherwise, not be inspired by that?

Eric Esquivel has written prose, comic books, stage plays, video games, and even the occasional mea culpa.

A Tale of Acceptable Loss
by D.A. Gray

Organizers planned a parade
   for the coming extinction
though we called it something else,
   even decorated with flags.
A counterprotest formed on the margins
   where children demanded
potable water, women access
   to healthcare, and everyone
the right to set the course
   of their lives and to not
be shot for it.
   In the center, rumor
spread like bacteria
   which was all it took
to stir up the rage.
   Where the people met
someone held an image in the air.
   It was a modern version
of Hicks' "Peaceable Kingdom"
  and the words
We thrive together or We perish together.
   The sign enraged the celebrants
who shouted, Nature will not replace us!
   Before the tear gas
the cameras cut away and the station
   brought in a scientist
who speculated the cost of inaction
   in terms of lives,
while a politician across the desk
   responded, Well, OK,
long as it's someone else's child.

D. A. Gray is the author of Contested Terrain *(FutureCycle Press, 2017). His poems have appeared in* The Sewanee Review, Still: The Journal, Appalachian Heritage, St. Katherine Review, Collateral Journal, *and* The Wrath-Bearing Tree. *He earned a Master of Fine Arts at the Sewanee School of Letters. A retired soldier, Gray now teaches, writes, and lives in Central Texas.*

Dust Bowl Revisited
by Herb Kauderer

The second devastation
of the Kansas ecology
was not from over-farming,
or aliens, or nuclear fallout,
and not even water pollution.
Civilization ran
the Ogallala Aquifer
out of water.

What followed was the resurrection
of dryland farming methods
and the creation of so many
new dry farming methods,
that the growing of food
on the surface of Mars
outside the domes, flourished.
And that's how
the capital of Mars came to be
named Kansas City.

Herb Kauderer has had thousands of poems published, and received many accolades for them. He is a retired factory worker/truck driver who grew up to become a tenured associate professor of English at Hilbert College. His doctoral dissertation was on Anglo-Canadian science-fiction. He lives at the northeast corner of Lake Erie, where the winters are cruel.

The Perpetual Lonesomeness
of Reincarnation
by Chase Dimock

I sometimes believe, in a previous life,
I read your treatise on irrigation by kerosene lamp,
and its empirical evidence, modern geometries
burst through tradition, opened dimensions,
spoke to something, squeaking like a baby bird
in my stomach, hungry for a world yet to exist.

I had to write you, though I knew nothing of farming,
channeling river tributaries, or the annual yield
of sorghum per barrel. I only knew, somewhere
on a dusty plain, you saw the potential of Eden,
a future beyond the horizon, infinite fertility
in an era when men kept their eyes on their straight
and narrow plow lines: a path from crib to crypt.

We corresponded, and you took it upon yourself
to educate me on agronomy and wrote effusively,
passionate for the endless potential for hybridization.
And yet, between the commas, I felt a sigh
nobody else could register, after each period,
a desire cut off by the grammar of decency.

I tried to keep up, borrowed every book from the library,
memorized the tables in the Farmer's Almanac,
wondered what it would be like to see the sunrise with you
on June 25th, 1874 predicted at 6:14 a.m., lie with you
and watch your well-watered fields of wheat illuminate
from dark purple to golden waves of genius.

Somewhere in your calculations,
you saw the future of skyscrapers, the bullet trains,
the disco ball's mirrored rainbow prisms
orbiting across our faces. Somewhere in the lazy loops
of your Os and Ls, you were diagramming
centuries in the future, how you hold me,
laying on the couch, watching our sleeping dog's
ampersand body breathing in and out.

When the letters stopped, I had no way of knowing why.
Maybe you found a young man, who could keep up
with your visions. Perhaps the Postmaster
finally understood my innuendos about laying pipes
and fed the pages to the furnace. Maybe Tuberculosis
finally reached the midwest, and I had no way of knowing
where to send the calla lilies you taught me
contain both male and female parts.

Today, I slump in front of my computer.
It's been 47 minutes since I sent my last text message.
You have yet to respond, and I feel like my stagecoach
has busted an axle. The children have diphtheria,
and the squirrel meat can only go so far.

I think of all the car accidents you have died in
since then, just to spite me.

I know you'll return the message, promptly
and eloquently as always. But until then,
I prepare your eulogy, open a window, let in a cold wind,
walk the widow's landing, and stare into the stars.
I imagine when I'll find you again: your transmissions
about terraforming on Mars stimulating my antenna.

Chase Dimock holds a doctorate in comparative literature from the University of Illinois, and teaches literature and writing in Los Angeles. He is the author of Sentinel Species *(Stubborn Mule Press, 2020), and the editor-in-chief of the on-line magazine* As It Ought To Be. *His poetry has previously appeared in* Rappahannock Review, Waccamaw, Connecticut River Review, Bombay Gin, Roanoke Review, *and* Little Patuxent Review, *among other magazines.*

Midwestern Gold
by Charlotte Brookins

Before I die, I imagine Iowa will smell like popcorn.

As I flee town on asphalt that cleaves through the Heartland like a teaspoon through half-warmed margarine, passing wind turbines with red eyes that blink like they know what I did when I was fourteen under the summer Missouri sky, the familiar aroma of cow shit and stale air will be usurped by the popping of corn. The eschatological flight of the sowers will replace the miasmic haze of death and fear and sweat with sticky cinemas that play disaster movies on loop, drive-ins that offer apologies for the wait and ask *didn't we go to the same elementary school?*

But outside the borders of my internal open-air film reel, I and everyone else will be long dead, either by heat stroke or hyperthermia or pyroclastic flows that boil soft tissue before the air reaches the necessary 400-degree range that will result in the exsanguination of those precious kernels. Apophenic church spires will reach with bulky, benighted arms up to God, and by the time He starts to conduct His final symphony, the crack-banging of maize will be our death knells, sounding off from the only ears left to listen. We will be buried beneath Midwestern gold, my body lying between the girl I named my first friend and the one who called me *dyke* in the sixth grade and I will struggle to tell them apart.

The only thing missing will be butter.

Charlotte Brookins is a Midwest-based writer who graduated from the University of Iowa with a degree in English and creative writing in 2024. Her work has been published internationally in such magazines as Haunted Words Press, All Existing, Wilder Things, *and more. When she's not reading, writing, or spending time with loved ones, she can be found getting lost in the woods.*

Flight Attendants
by Herb Kauderer

Iowa ethanol is the best for rocket fuel.

It pushes ships outside the atmosphere
with a meat and potatoes practicality

and a promise that humans
on the new L5 colony
will soon be outnumbered by hogs

four to one, just like the folks
making the fuel and sending the recipes

for making the best of the
sustainable food system they've got.

Herb Kauderer has had thousands of poems published, and received many accolades for them. He is a retired factory worker/truck driver who grew up to become a tenured associate professor of English at Hilbert College. His doctoral dissertation was on Anglo-Canadian science-fiction. He lives at the northeast corner of Lake Erie, where the winters are cruel.

Splashdown
by Randy Brown

I grew up on coastal rocket ships
collectible mission patches
and handshakes in space

But later my family hard-landed
onto a post-settlement, industrialized soil—

a strange new terrain
that has predicted itself

the future birthplace of James T. Kirk.

There's no Synthehol yet,
but I drink my corn nightly,

guessing at which stars
will be the ones to whoosh past—

swerving like headlights on farm roads
and opening credits on TV ...

Only some of us may "boldly go";
others gladly, boldly stay.

*Randy Brown traveled the world as a child in an active-duty U.S. Air Force
family in the 1970s, which included a stint on Florida's "Space Coast." After
mustering out in the '80s, the family landed permanently and happily in
Iowa. Brown is the editor of the 2024 anthology* Giant Robot Poems: On
Mecha-Human Science, Culture & War *(Middle West Press).*

SouLoans™
by Nayt Rundquist

Tristenne's been paying off her soul for years. It should've meant better jobs, houses, tech interfacing, but she's been scraping bottom to cover costs. One person ahead in line. She sold limbs for this final payment; soon she'll soul-tube across the galaxy. She'll finally live. She'll find Isolde.

WindowBot9000 gestures. Offering her hand, she winces at the drawn blood. OVERDUE flashes onscreen. PAY NOW? She punches yes, drops in credit sticks. PAYMENT ACCEPTED.

She steps aside, shrugs out of her body. As it slumps to the floor, she flutters off to find tech to hermit crab into and start anew.

Nayt Rundquist (they/them) is managing editor of The Kenyon Review. *Their odd scribblings can be found in* Inverted Syntax, Digging Through the Fat, Roi Fainéant, X-R-A-Y Lit Mag, Scavengers Lit Mag, The Citron Review, *and anthologized in* Unbound: Composing Home *(New Rivers Press, 2022) and* it always finds me *(Querencia Press, 2024). They live just outside space and time with their artist-jeweler wife and their fifth-dimensional dogs.*

It's Always All About the Weather in Greenfield, Iowa
by Robert Frazier

If I were the calm before the storm
My brain pan would crackle
With lightning strikes of recall
My worries form a distant thunder
My soul in a plains twister rotation
Would tear the door hinges off
Museums of my precognition
I would be the canary in the mine
A forecaster of future weathers
If I were the calm before the storm

Robert Frazier is a 3-time winner of the Rhysling Award, and the recipient of a 2005 Grandmaster Award, from the Science Fiction & Fantasy Poetry Association (SFPA).

Meet Me in Saint Louis (Lifecycle of a City)
by Benjamin B. White

The Gashouse Gang was fun to watch
And soon after, #6 hit .331 lifetime,
But all pastimes pass in the silencing
        Of the crowd's last cheer
And the gateway to the frontier
Was just where Trans World Airlines
Went out of business in a leaky airport
Handling the baggage of a city's
        Decline and decay
As brick warehouse prosperity
Gave way to be boarded up
And replaced by nostalgia
Served with hole-in-the-wall chow mein
        And the pain of neglect
In neighborhoods full
Of select Judy Garland mansions
Abandoned in a sad musical depiction
Of the blues floating by
Letting simplicity turn complex
        With social attitudes and fear
Reflected in a glistening tear
Rolling down the cheek of Americana
Hoping to still be kissed by tourists
Crammed into a corner down by the river
        With a casino and the Arch
Trying to resurrect the adventurous spirit
Of mountain men and trappers
Headed west into the vast emptiness
That has creeped back east
To become downtown

In a sad, slow commute unable
To reclaim or silence history
Where the future has moved into the suburbs
For comfort and safety
Watching the city crumble
All around itself
    And its loss of importance.

Benjamin B. White is the author of five poetry collections including: God is an Atheist *(Alien Buddha Press, 2024) and* Always Ready: Poems from a Life in the U.S. Coast Guard *(Middle West Press, 2022). He is also the author of* The Recon Trilogy + 1 *(Running Wild Press, 2020), a collection of four Iliad-like narrative poems in modern military milieu.*

When the mayor tells us to shower with a buddy
by Bethany Tap

Will it be spring, like before, the Grand River overflowing her banks? We'll see fish swimming past the windows of office buildings. Steelhead salmon, silver-scaled and red-bellied, barely flopping to ascend the fish ladder, continuing the journey home. Mornings we'll wake to water. Water at our doors, pleading for entry, puddled on our floors, dripping from ceilings, clutching pruny fingers around the foundations of our homes, opening greedy mouths gushing-wide to devour cars, dribbling smiles washing out bridges, roads. We'll always try to give her a wide berth, but the rain keeps falling, the river keeps rising, we keep raging: these are our homes, our things. Ours. A duck paddles across the neighbor's lawn and he shoots it. What else can he do? We'll be told to stay home, conserve water, and respect the river. Knee-deep in our wet former-lawns we will wander and wonder at the landscape transformed, at this brave new watery world, at the assumption we've always held: that we are the masters, that any of this is ours. We will stand and wait until the river crests, the rain stops, the waters fall, and we can forget again.

Bethany Tap is a queer writer living in Grand Rapids, Michigan with her wife and four kids. Recent publications include poems in Emerge Literary Journal *and* Yellow Arrow Journal, *and fiction in* NonBinary Review *and* Flash Frontier. *Visit: bethanytap.com*

The Day the Trees Retaliate
by Wendy BooydeGraaff

Gentle giants, silent, strong
roots reach long into leaf

decay, leaching minerals
soil old as dirt

roads rutted by wagon
wheels. Older. Cousins

relegated within sophisticated
steel skirts on city hills,

grown pool-side, ambient
sparkle lights, trimmed to limit

shade, removed completely
when leaves litter

swimming water. Clog eaves.
What if, the tree,

awakened from its peaceful
stoicism, reaches out a sharp

twig, slices off a finger. *Too
close*, it says. A root snakes up,

strangles an ankle. *Don't steal
my water*. Leaves whip

an entire human to a new
location. Time for renovation.

A hard fruit knocked upon
a hard head, unconscious, flat

upon the soil. *Better*. Allow
the sunlight in. The ticking

of the tree against aluminum
siding, a bomb. People

burned, uprooted, trimmed back,
replaced with thinner, younger

versions—trees who absorbed
human ways rather than the other

way round.

Wendy BooydeGraaff's fiction, poems, and essays have been published in Phoebe, Cutleaf, Slag Glass City, *and* Slant: A Journal of Poetry. *Born and raised in Ontario, Canada, she now lives in Michigan.*

When the East was won
by Beau Brockett

Clinton Township's big enough for the two of us
but sometimes it feels like it ain't.

Down in the old basement bar
my pa's always reminiscin'

'bout the cafeteria that used to be
in the factory, and the softball leagues,

—teams and teams—and the old haunt
they'd mosey over to when they lost.

How did those good ol' boys work
for so much goodness and let it fall to this?

A ghost township of strips
and subdivisions, a cemetery inheritance

that keeps tumbleweedin' out.
Come here. Look out.

'Member what this cul-de-sac
used to be? A desert of cowboys

and Indians. The place you'd count to twenty
and then seek me. We took the street,

the yards, and made 'em ours. Do you
still feel that at times, that rumblin' of somethin'

better? It's like creaky knee meteorology,
and I wanna lasso that storm inside me.

The East was won
property line by property line.

So what say we ransack Meijer's another time.
You can quick draw the blunt and sting me

a hit under parking lot lamp light.
Then we can take Roxy

outta Maple Ridge to a real maple ridge
tonight. Take 'er past 25 Mile, 26,

'til they stop keepin' count.
We can lie in the cargo bed, untether

ourselves, and dream uppa big stickup:
a mall, an old field, a trailer park.

Let's break free like them KFC workers
break across these six-lane roads toward home.

You and me, partner.
Let's stake our own.

*Beau Brockett's hometown is tucked between the sprawl of Metro Detroit,
and the crops and coast of Michigan's Thumb—a liminal space of sorts with
strip-malls and rural mentalities creeping in on both sides. "Places that
people purposely move to, that people are stuck in, and that people want to
make better." He seeks to bring humanity and wonder back into such places.*

A Little Home in Lake Forest
by Melle Graihagh

Flora Shingalls moved to the wild frontier with her Ma and Pa and Mara and Baby Sherry. That morning Ma had woken the girls early and handed them each a microwavable breakfast burrito wrapped in 1-ply paper towel. Flora pouted because half of hers was still cold, but Mara obediently ate hers and neatly threw the paper towel in the plastic bag hanging on the handle of the pantry door. The family loaded into a Toyota Corolla that should be white but was mostly reddish-orange.

"Pa," Flora cried from the middle back seat, "I don't wanna leave Wisconsin." Pa looked at Flora through the rearview mirror and winked at her. "If we stay, my 'little half-pint half-drunk-up' will be filled with radium water. And no one wants a brew quite like that."

"Karls!" Ma admonished, but Pa just shot her a sly smile and grabbed her hand across the center console.

Ma, Pa, Flora, Mara, and Baby Sherry arrived in Iowa after a long 10-hour drive. "I believe we've found the perfect place! Lake Forest!" Pa announced. The quaint neighborhood was half mobile homes, half ruins, like a dream only partially imagined. "A tornado hit this village two months ago and we're free to claim this land for our own."

That night Ma pulled out sleeping bags and the Shingalls family slept in the parking lot. For the first time in her life, Flora saw the stars.

Pa's rich baritone lulled her to sleep:

My life flows on in endless song,
above earth's lamentation.
I catch the sweet, though far-off hymn
that hails a new creation.

Through all the tumult and the strife,
I hear that music ringing.
It finds an echo in my soul.
How can I keep from singing?

Melle Graihagh is a Canadian-born author living in South Carolina with her two cats. In her spare time, she enjoys content creation, reading, and video games—and, occasionally, all three at once!

AP Biochem, Class of 2035
by N. Jed Todd

Well, I don't think you need to—
    Pardon me, can you stick out your tongue? Aah? Does it hurt?
    And what about here? Hmm, how much?
Put that down for mild adverse.

What was I saying? Oh yes, don't be shy,
All of these will one day be where you are
As you were once where they—
    Can you turn and cough? Once more?
    Oh dear. For constipation? That one will never work.
Mark that failure.

And you once were where they are now ...
No? You got the scholarship without
Without high school work study?
Must be nice to have parents in important places.
Let me explain a little, then ...
    Oh that looks very fine,
    Very fine indeed
Minimal edema, mark that a success.

But to explain to our bright-eyed intern ...
Between AI and quantum simulations
Drug discovery is ever-so-elegant and quick
And without a need for painstaking trial-and-error

Until it comes to side-effects
For that we need a little human trial
Especially for the psychoactives
To quantify what exhaustive lists of receptor subtypes cannot

And see just how much to save for settlements

So we take these high school boys and girls
And give them—
    I see your vitals are running very high,
    Temp and heart and maybe even diastolic
    How long has this been going on?
    Hmm. What was the dosage?
Let's reduce that on the next trial,
Try half an m-l twice daily

And those that get the credit, well,
It looks great on a college application
Not to mention twice minimum wage,
Almost enough for school fees
When we partner with our charter schools

And, as you well know, our corporate scholarship program
Is nothing to sneeze—
    Oh dear. You've been doing that how long?
    Can you blink a bit for me?
Take that down for an animal model
If it doesn't go away
And maybe critical life-saving interventions
If it goes away with time

Isn't corporate biochemistry exciting?
We remake the world in our best image
Or at least spread a bit more widely
All our worst fever dreams.

N. Jed Todd is a father, husband, retired U.S. Army master sergeant, and a Texan, in that order. As a Russian linguist working in Signals Intelligence and Psychological Operations, he served in Bosnia, Afghanistan, Iraq, Kuwait, Cyprus, Mali, and Central Africa, not necessarily in that order. His wife, Ami, and daughter, Meera, tolerate him in no order at all. He works now for the U.S. Air Force Futures office on the Information Warfare Capability Development Team. His work has previously appeared in the anthology Giant Robot Poems: On Mecha-Human Culture, Science & War *(Middle West Press, 2024), and in the Science Fiction & Fantasy Poetry Association's on-line journal* Eye to the Telescope.

Stealing Raspberry Kisses
by Maggs Vibo

Corn-fed cattle rattle inside their steel boxes
Wages stagnate again. Half-baked urgencies and securities
Dirty, like when we were children
And would eat mud cakes and dirt pies
A memory of you traipsing along our pond, not far from Honey Creek
Holding a handful of cattails and stealing wild raspberries
Giggling. Hands red-stained. Still, you lied.
Lips ready like a largemouth bass
Harmless fish tales. To hell with facts!
Back before autonomous wars scarred the fields with ash
Back when the soil was rich in Iowa
When we'd barefoot-wander—never considering landmines
Before the age of tracking devices
And satellites scanning our whereabouts
We'd walkabout and play pretend. Spend hours and days
Dreaming in the sunshine. Running round the barns carefree
We'd ride bikes on gravel roads and play Duck, Duck, Goose
It's against policy now to step from domicile detentions
We smile, but our eyes bear the burden of our trespasses
Our air contaminated, yet filtered
Formulated and calibrated to give just enough
Our sustenance bagged, tagged, and we gag on protein
Bars
Our harnessed reality
Everything produced to provide just the right amount of fuel
So, you'll sneak across the Missouri to steal berries
Wrinkled hands marked by impulsivity
You'll hide the stains while in line for accountability
Try to dodge the pesticides that remain in your blood
'til a company sample provides ample proof that

You're the face of the resistance
Still, you'll insist your sister had nothing to do with it
And I'm innocent except for the scans of my dilated pupils
Excited by the memories of life before this robotic jail
Cuffed, they'll name me Huckle-Bearer
As your remains dangle from within a steel box
Chained round my red wrists
A sample of life when there's no ducking

Maggs Vibo is a visual poet and U.S. Army veteran residing in Vicenza, Italy, while her spouse is attached to U.S. Army's Southern European Task Force, Africa (SETAF-AF). Her latest art can be found at the Dulles International Airport gallery through 2027. Past exhibitions include Honolulu Printmakers, L'Air Arts at Atelier 11 in Paris, and both the Embassy of the United Kingdom and Library of Congress in Washington, D.C. She has contributed to dozens of anthologies, including Maintenant 18: A Journal of Contemporary Dada Writing and Art *(Three Rooms Press, 2024). Visit: maggsvibo.com*

We'll Still Be Here
by Zackary Ross Wiggs

When the sun pops
The corn in its husk …

When the tornadoes
Strip it all clean again…

When the stars
are gated neighborhoods …

When the locusts
Finally fall silent…

When dust chokes
The Midwest skies again …

When the last
Dollar Store boards up …

Zackary Ross Wiggs is a writer from southeast Kansas. Writing genre fiction and poetry, he has previously been published in places like Shacklebound Press, The New Verse News, *and* Bullshit Lit. *When not writing, he's usually found near the edge of the Ozarks with his partner and their cat.*

Minneapolis 2064
by Casey Fuller

There will be trees
many many trees
trees like the trees
they said we'd see
when we closed our
eyes to the bright light
of what we once could
see as ideal. Words
will once again regain
the luster of what
we first thought they
referred to. No one
will be pulled over
for a bulb gone out
in a taillight or for
passing a fake twenty.
Phone vids will not
come into flood our
streams in ways that
feel unbearable and
uncontrollable through
devices we hold close
to our bodies. The painting
of William Blake
where people swirl up
to heaven into song
won't appear as
the first flash of
a fire blast before
a 2,000-pound bomb

vaporizes poor people
off the face of the earth.
Some dreams will disappear.
The world won't reverse
but become re-regular,
non-romantic, un-visionary.
A time will reoccur
when you can walk again
and breathe again
with no fires hazing
the horizon nor haunting
the air with phantom films
of brown-yellow smoke.
The right forests will be
on fire. Your garden will grow
in old ways in bright green.
Where the sky starts will be
seen again. Regular wind
will undulate real limbs
very softly. And there
will be trees. Many trees.
There will be many, many trees.

Casey Fuller is a doctoral student in English at the University of North Dakota. His poems have appeared in journals, a chapbook, and an anthology entitled Nothing to Declare: A Guide to the Flash Sequence. *In 2023, he received the Thomas McGrath Award. He has a cat named Garcia Lorca.*

Robinia Pseudoacacia (commonly black locust)
by Bethany Tap

Our backyard tree, that's her name: white-flowered not-acacia, with toxic black-hearted pods. *Black locust*. The arborist who's come to trim her leans back, admiring her reach. *Biggest I've ever seen*, wider than the circling reach of two adults. In spring, she drops spiked offerings. Her thorns slice our soles. Her trunk absorbed old cables, exposed plastic and wire bits like strange piercings. Somewhere within her bosom, where her branches curve into her trunk, a mama raccoon built a nest. *Invasive species*, according to the DNR, displaying tawdry photos of her sprawled-open pods, finger-like leaves cajoling, the pure white blush of sweet-pea flowers. Her root systems sprawl beneath our yard, an intricate colony awakening each year to spread. We pull up suckling sprouts but the infestation is here, here, and here. We cannot stymy her. She is every conquering deity, thrumming city, worming cancer, seductive whisper, feared, loved, loathed, and worshipped.

Bethany Tap is a queer writer living in Grand Rapids, Michigan with her wife and four kids. Recent publications include poems in Emerge Literary Journal *and* Yellow Arrow Journal, *and fiction in* NonBinary Review *and* Flash Frontier. *Visit: bethanytap.com*

Underneath this surface
by Mahaila Smith

(A "Sporror" subgenre poem loosely inspired by Histoplasma fungus,
which was concentrated in the Midwest in the 1950s and '60s.)

My reflection looks back
from the pockmarked glass of muddy ice.
I touch ice dark lines in my skin,
splintered and runic.
A face both new and heart-rending.
I scrape hard-packed snow
against my cheeks. The markings stay.
Sat beneath the surface.
I did not escape in time.
Tendrils of the aggressive microfungi
weave new internal networks
finding a way to continue to spread.
I had hoped to walk towards the next town
or the next. To find somewhere
the hyphae lost.
I condemn myself to solitude.
To wait to die where no one can breathe
these poisonous spores, smaller than dust.

Mahaila Smith (any pronouns) is a young femme writer, living and working on the traditional territory of the Algonquin Anishinabeg in Ottawa, Ontario. They are one of the co-editors for The Sprawl Mag. Their chapbooks include Water-Kin (Metatron Press, 2024) and Enter the Hyperreal (above/ground press, 2024). Their novelette in verse, Seed Beetle, is forthcoming with Stelliform Press. Visit: mahailasmith.ca

This meager recompense
by Mahaila Smith

(A "Sporror" subgenre poem loosely inspired by Histoplasma fungus,
which was concentrated in the Midwest in the 1950s and '60s.)

I am cold to my bones.
Snow melt has trickled
beneath my fur under the rock ledge.
I remove my socks,
wring them out with shaking hands
and bury them under precious dried leaves.
I allow myself one small luxury.
I take a mug from the ground,
bring it down to the river.
I collect a bough of pine,
stripping the green needles
and stuffing them in my pocket.
I scoop a current of river water
and set it on the bank.
I clear a spot on the ground,
bring leaves and dried branches,
squirreled away under the ledge.
I pile them up.
Take the matchbook from a pocket,
and drag a match against the striker paper.
I hold it against the kindling. Watch it light.
I build the flame until it's fierce.
You arrive—invader,
as I am placing my cup
of water and needles
into the flame.
I hold out the handle to you first.

You take it with your shaking hand.
The fungi has marked your fingers,
with its coded script.
It doesn't matter,
but it also matters more than anything in the world.

Mahaila Smith (any pronouns) is a young femme writer, living and working on the traditional territory of the Algonquin Anishinabeg in Ottawa, Ontario. They are one of the co-editors for The Sprawl Mag. Their chapbooks include Water-Kin (Metatron Press, 2024) and Enter the Hyperreal (above/ground press, 2024). Their novelette in verse, Seed Beetle, is forthcoming with Stelliform Press. Visit: mahailasmith.ca

A place to rest
by Mahaila Smith

*(A "Sporror" subgenre poem loosely inspired by Histoplasma fungus,
which was concentrated in the Midwest in the 1950s and '60s.)*

The river splits around a fallen trunk,
whitewater wavering and dipping.
The shore is bordered with snow-capped stones,
spilling down to ripple the riverbed.

Like me, the trees around are slivered with rot.
Gaping black cavities expose
cross sections of years turned to pulp.
The growth of centuries, lost to parasite.
I press a finger into decaying sapwood,
tawny splinters sticking to my finger pad.

The water crashes then whispers,
repeating its unending trek,
bound to the coast of chronic snow.
I dig my nails into the wood,
and feel no needling in my nail bed.

Mahaila Smith (any pronouns) is a young femme writer, living and working on the traditional territory of the Algonquin Anishinabeg in Ottawa, Ontario. They are one of the co-editors for The Sprawl Mag. Their chapbooks include Water-Kin (Metatron Press, 2024) and Enter the Hyperreal *(above/ground press, 2024). Their novelette in verse,* Seed Beetle, *is forthcoming with Stelliform Press. Visit: mahailasmith.ca*

Under Soft Rains
by Zebulon Huset

Cityfolks likely knew why the sky went orange, but back in these parts, isolated by both mountains and ocean, we don't get much news. First darkness under black clouds, then ash rain for thirty weeks, now the fiery orange sky every day. Corn, beans and taters still grew fine, maybe a mite small. Once the snow fell and melted it washed away most of the ash. We grew some bumps, coughed more than we remembered, found more dead gulls than normal, but for the most part life rolled on. Cityfolks might have it different, maybe even harder, but ... their troubles have always been their own.

Zebulon Huset is a high school teacher, writer and photographer. He won the Gulf Stream 2020 Summer Poetry Contest and his writing has appeared in Best New Poets, Meridian, North American Review, The Southern Review, Fence, *and* Gone Lawn, *among others. He publishes the blog Notebooking Daily, and edits the literary journal* Coastal Shelf.

The Prairie
by Casey Fuller

after Susan Stewart

You should wake now to remember the prairie. For it is reappearing as
    we run our eyes
over the words. It may be false to imagine what you only fly over:
    so what details we place

in the erasure might feel like a flower crown laurelling the brow
    of the dead. A death we imagined,
yes, since it's one that circulates in memory, so we might call it
    "un-remembering the prairie."

You should rise now and un-remember the prairie,
    for, in that recollection, you might
rearrange it to "just above the prairie." See how the falsity begins
    in present, ending

somewhere where these words start to end, infecting that first layer,
    the anti-place where
memory shines brightly, that ash. (Not the treasure house you dreamt
    of, but the gray-scape

where you honestly spend most of your life wandering in your mind,
    which, oddly feels firm,
footed, empiric, for that place is inside a river, nevertheless, you could
    call it "of the prairie,"

where no one can truly drift below, no oil resides, no person, no town is
    drowned by a dam.)
And gray in life, too, lost in the first layer, to that anti-place you dis-
    remember, a flower crown

circling your own head, black oil there, as if footed, firm, empiric,
  for that place is a river,
like a windrower mowing down grass from the land. Meadowlarks
  and blackbirds flute

above and below where no oil resides, no person, no town is drowned
  by a poorly planned dam.
And gray in life, too, flute and twitter beyond a pale rage for order,
  circulating in time,

that ash, where river rocks glisten under a crosshatch of broken
  branches, where the air
is scent-flecked with fresh hay, the meadowlarks and black birds flute
  above and below,

a musk of smoke circling the pale air. They flute a song beyond the rage
  for order, enskyed:
everything flies over us here. Where the air is scent-fleck with fresh hay
  (in the place

we are landed) the prairie is redacted, in a mixed musk of diesel
  and impending cold, beside
a catchment of brown brambles, ice-still and blue starred, tall grass
  and silver sage, prairie

clover and wild rye, a blue plastic bottle—everything flies over us here,
  stainless.
No branch can swing above a brook in a place we weren't born,
  the prairie was redacted,

no enclosure can stop the width running in all directions. You can
  understand what I'm saying
when I tell you an endlessness runs all ways at once—the way tallgrass
  and silver sage, prairie

clover and wild rye, a plastic bag from a superstore—is not a kind
of limit. Sometimes I imagine us
lying down looking up at the planes flying above us (... tallgrass and
silver sage, no branch above

the brook in the place we weren't raised) in a space that is nothing like
the prairie. But certainly
we can imagine a truer place, where the real ground is covered
(you can understand

what I'm telling you when I say endlessness runs all directions at once)
by needlegrass,
by common cattail—nothing acts as a kind of limit. And slow below the
leaves of grass,

bleached in the alkaline salt shallows, a system of roots. But certainly we
can see the other place,
also, where the ground is covered in steaming windrows of upturned
land, so grave-like,

so life-giving, also, by needlegrass, by common cattail. We were once
found in the prairie,
so circled in, and yet so grave-like and upturned, too, but the truth is,
it is founded in us now.

*Casey Fuller is a doctoral student in English at the University of North
Dakota. His poems have appeared in journals, a chapbook, and 2016
anthology* Nothing to Declare: A Guide to the Flash Sequence *(White
Pine Press). He has a cat named Garcia Lorca. Fuller received the 2023
Thomas McGrath Award for "The Prairie."*

A Walk in the Park
by Tucker Struyk

As sandhill cranes roosted in the sandbar and black-tailed prairie dogs foraged for Western wheatgrass, a lone doe ambled through Clift Park. Picnic tables and park benches sat empty after the evacuation left the city entombed in forgotten legacy. In the light of day, when the foxes and coyotes rested on full bellies, deer had the lay of the land. She noshed on the leaves of giant ragweed and snuffled the flowering blooms of chicory weeds. Without the incessant spray of herbicide, lamb's quarters blossomed under the red maple canopy—which provided nourishment for the fawns of spring. Though, not all the babes lived to see the summer sun. Some were born with fatal congenital disorders that stripped a doe of her motherhood. As she moseyed down a slope to sip from the confluence of streams at her hooves, the mourning dove cooed overhead. The doe tilted her head toward the turtledove, then to the ashen aurorae on the horizon.

Tucker Struyk (he/him/his) is a queer writer and podcaster for Hookswitch Hotline. He has pieces published by Cosmic Horror Monthly, A Coup of Owls, Eerie River Publishing, *and several other publications. His piece "Our Father's Judgment" was published in the spring 2021 issue of* 13th Floor Magazine, *where it was awarded an Editor's Choice Award. His piece "Getaway" achieved an honorable mention in the Fall/Winter 2022-23 issue of* Allegory.

The Hunting of the Flarks
by Herb Kauderer

> *"The Bandersnatch fled as the others appeared*
> *Led on by that fear-stricken yell:*
> *And the Bellman remarked 'it is just as I feared!'*
> *And solemnly tolled on his bell"*
> —Lewis Carroll

When the aquatic Flarks invaded,
Nebraska was about the safest place to be.
Far from the coasts,
The Great Plains gave the locals
plenty of time to see the foreign submersibles
rising out of deep lakes and rivers.
Not that the Nebraskans weren't used to keeping an eye out
for all their homegrown cryptids,
the Walgren Lake Monster, the Lake Ogallala Monster,
and the Aurora Witch, who is more of a ghost
than a cryptid proper. They were ready
for every kind of hunt, even for Flarks.
As the war continued it became clear
that the greatest weapon against the aliens was cold.
So, humans reversed global warming. With their guns
safely stored they hosed the aliens with cold fronts and ice
with hail and blizzards, with sleet and freezing rain.
The thing about the locals is they know
when it's too cold for school, or work, or hunting.
In snug bungalows and ranches
blackout curtains were hung to keep the heat in.
Americans banded together, red and blue,
to freeze the grey skin of the Flarks into white.
They put to use all the self-coping
and entertainments they learned

during the last pandemic. In the end, exterminating
a sentient race was not the happy resolution
of global warming that anyone expected
but having a common enemy never fails.
And cozied inside with hot toddies and mulled wine
the Cornhuskers said prayers that the cryptids survived
so that hunting would return when the long winter ended.

Herb Kauderer has had thousands of poems published, and received many accolades for them. He is a retired factory worker/truck driver who grew up to become a tenured associate professor of English at Hilbert College. His doctoral dissertation was on Anglo-Canadian science-fiction. He lives at the northeast corner of Lake Erie, where the winters are cruel.

The Green Man of Akron
by Joseph Phelan

We emerged from the lobby's glacial climate, man and dog, to stroll along the offramp knolls—heeding nature's call. Addled thoughts dissolved into purpling dusk and twenty-one hindleg salutes. Crossing the soft green berm into a maze of silent side streets, we're drawn like moths toward truculent lighting.

Nearly the last night of spring, Ohio air, floral and mossy, alive with possibility and rhyming with the wag of a loping white tail, we follow that persistent snout—confident in its quest for goose droppings in the dark.

Our kindred souls are sensitive and rational, our auras haloed by mayflies. The murmur of cars becomes hard to distinguish from the distant fall of crooked Cuyahoga. The tightening leash alerts me that we've ventured too far.

Commercial lease available, Embassy Parkway Pavilions, a cove of mirrored glass geodes encircling tar-veined asphalt and flickering amber lampposts. Probably all empty these days. But the once articulate landscaping is rewilding, atavistic and, seemingly, pregnant.

Fear begets fear. They smell it too. Hungover breakout session crowds and the pitbull that stalked us along Birmingham Road in Virginia.

A perfect lair—a void abhorred by the lost people and broken men.

Perhaps returning now, in bands, to the Ohio forests of their forebears.

This was once the great northwestern wilderness, after all. Washington camped on the banks of the Ohio and wild Ulstermen dug canals along Indian footpaths, beneath the primeval canopy. A squirrel could bound from branch to branch, from the Atlantic across Appalachia, unto the shores of Erie, Huron and Michigan, without ever once touching the ground. An arboreal rodent superhighway.

I fear the fentanyl and methamphetamine, animism among recyclables. Still, to be renewed as a pioneer in the parallel apocalypse?

Writing ballads? New campfire songs for the ancient of days?

Moisture growing in my grip, pulsations in my periphery, someone loomed and leered, menacing limbs suggested by the rustling hostas.

Where the sidewalk stopped, a shrouded grotto spotted, a tent near the power box?

Let's get out of here.

If we make it back to the cool sheets, with life and leash in hand, we'll drink deeply and gratefully, bottled water splashed into the ice bucket top. We'll wake, ourselves again, under the reassuring tiles of an acoustic ceiling.

Joe Phelan writes from the western suburbs of Chicago, where he lives with his wife, sons, and intrepid rescue mutt. Whenever possible, he escapes with them to the Northwoods of Wisconsin. Phelan's work has appeared in Ekstasis Magazine, Maudlin House, *and* After Hours. *The flash "The Green Man of Akron" originally appeared in Issue No. 37 of* LIT *Magazine. Visit: joephelan.net*

Arctic Winds in Wisconsin
by F. Malanoche

My mother always
Said there are no snow
Days in adulthood.

Thirty years later,
I huddle under
My cotton bed sheets.

Wind rattles the walls
Of my apartment
As the ground water
Freezes with a pop!

Heated blankets do
Little to slow the
Cold, so we turn on
The open oven.

The view through the glass
Is a snow globe, an
Upside down world in
A blanket of white.

The anchorman warns
Against the outdoors.
Ice snaps the power
Lines, and all goes dark.

F. Malanoche writes, under the cover of night, hoping to bring authentic and odd Latino stories into the world. He teaches English in the Midwest, has a wonderful wife, and a sweet vinyl collection. His writing has been published in Demonic Workplaces *(4 Horsemen Publications, 2023) and* Darkness 101: Lessons Were Learned *(Collective Tales Publishing, 2023). You can follow him at his Facebook page.*

White Stripes
by Eric Chandler

I want to write about
a dystopia in the future

I'll write about how I'll cross-country ski
for a whole season in my town

on a
White stripe of manmade snow

because no natural snow
will fall from the sky

I'll try three times in a whole winter
to cross-country ski

on something other than a
White stripe of manmade snow

but ninety percent of the time will be spent
skiing around like a hamster on a wheel

on that
White stripe of manmade snow

I'll write about how one winter
a major anniversary of a famous ski marathon

will happen on a carefully built
White stripe of manmade snow

and that will coincide with the major anniversary
of my, let's say, twentieth time skiing in that event

and then I'll imagine that the World Cup of cross-country skiing
comes to Minneapolis from Europe and the best skiers in the world

will come to the USA and go around and around on a
White stripe of manmade snow

I'll increase the tension by making it seem like
the event might get canceled due to the lack of even manmade snow

but I'll write that one of the only snowstorms of the year
will blanket the venue with flakes

and the crystals will shine in the sun as they race on the
White stripe of manmade snow

the spectators will be forgiven for not realizing that
the natural snow is just a lucky decoration and not the racing surface

and then I'll create a scenario where my college-age daughter
will travel to a collegiate national championships in, let's say,
     Lake Placid

where they have carefully preserved a
White stripe of manmade snow

that will nearly melt down in the forty-degree temperatures
I'll write that puddles form in the track and cause skiers to fall

I'll marvel at the venue and the new ski lodge and the
ski trail that has built-in snowmaking guns that

hover over the
White stripe of manmade snow

I'll invent a time, let's say, forty years earlier
when I skied on natural snow over the same trails
    where my daughter raced

I want to write about
this dystopia in the future

but there's one problem:
all of those things already happened last winter

I still want to write about
a dystopia in the future

indoor "ski tunnels" already exist in Europe
but I'll write that they build bleachers in one of these facilities

so people can pay to come watch a spectacle performed on a
White stripe of manmade snow

I'll be an old man who sells tickets to the spectators
so they can sit and watch a rarely seen activity

after the people fill the bleachers
I'll put on a pair of these things called "cross-country skis"

which can only be used within a concrete ski tunnel that refrigerates a
White stripe of manmade snow

because there will be no ski trails outside anymore
because it won't get cold enough to even make snow outside anymore

I'll skate ski past the bleachers and
I'll diagonal stride past the bleachers and

the people will laugh with amazement and point at the old timer
    gliding over the
White stripe of manmade snow

like someone giving a demonstration of how to spin yarn
an activity that nobody does anymore

like going to a historic fort at a national park
where the reenactors line up and pretend to fight a historic battle

the old man will reenact the ancient gliding ritual across the
White stripe of manmade snow

the old man will ignore the people in the bleachers and imagine
    being outside
skiing across the country for miles and miles and miles and miles.

Eric Chandler is the author of Kekekabic *(Finishing Line Press, 2022) and* Hugging This Rock *(Middle West Press, 2017). His writing has appeared in* Northern Wilds, Grey Sparrow Journal, The Talking Stick, Sleet Magazine, O-Dark-Thirty, Line of Advance, Collateral Journal, The Deadly Writers Patrol, PANK, The Wrath-Bearing Tree, Consequence Forum, *and* Columbia Journal. *He's happiest when he's on a trail in Duluth, Minnesota with his wife, two children, and faithful dog, Leo.*

Invasive Species
by D.A. Gray

We speak of life as something good in itself,
the word sparking images of green fields,
tall trees, lakes filled to the brim.
From a distance even the yard filled with weeds
seems to flourish, and the sick neighbor
who says only, "fine," when asked—his words can
be taken at face value.
                    And the lakes, when we're careless
dazzle us with the rainbows skimming the surface.

And this stand of catclaw vine feasting on the fallen
then moving on, wrapping itself around, choking,
the living. It never seems to be an invasion
when you're hungry. Until we reach ground level
hard to see a problem at all. From a distance it's just
life ascending (like cancer), high as the eyes can see.

D.A. Gray is the author of Contested Terrain *(FutureCycle Press, 2017).
His poems have appeared in* The Sewanee Review, Still: The Journal,
Appalachian Heritage, St. Katherine Review, Collateral Journal, *and*
The Wrath-Bearing Tree. *He earned a Master of Fine Arts at the Sewanee
School of Letters. A retired soldier, Gray now teaches, writes, and lives in
Central Texas.*

Texas Innovation
by N. Jed Todd

There is a market for weather derivatives, did you know?
A way to insure that even though the rain falls
On the just and unjust alike
It still profits mostly the rich
And well-connected

It's an ENRON product, one of their great innovations,
At least the ones not charged criminally,
And now it's a multi-million-dollar market.
Farmers get to insure their crops
If they've capital to spare
Instead of paying down interest
On their debt

But mostly it's insurance companies and hedge funds
Making sure that they still make money
Even when the winds and storms
Make life hard for the unprotected
Money can be a great insulator
Against climate change

And it occurs to me that out there, somewhere, alive this very day
Is the first guy to be convicted for insider trading
Against climate change. And you know it's a guy.
Some East Coast Ivy-League legacy in a suit
As expensive as the farmer's pickup truck
In whom he "invests."

And he's stood up in court or Congress and gave testimony
Of all the reasons climate change science
Is doubtable, debatable, indebted

And all the reasons why his company
Cannot be forced to indemnify
For what they've done.

While on the record that really counts, the bank ledger,
He put out bets to make sure that come what may
Come storm or drought or hail or fire
He was careful to follow the science
All the way to the bank

And ten-years in to a once-in-a-hundred-year drought
With the Panhandle worn-off and cracked
Like it was hung out over the fire
Instead of the copper-bottom
Of his careful investments
Just wrung dry

Like a stone drained of all its blood
By the fist of God
Isn't Texas innovation grand?

N. Jed Todd is a father, husband, retired U.S. Army master sergeant, and a Texan, in that order. As a Russian linguist working in Signals Intelligence and Psychological Operations, he served in Bosnia, Afghanistan, Iraq, Kuwait, Cyprus, Mali, and Central Africa, not necessarily in that order. His wife, Ami, and daughter, Meera, tolerate him in no order at all. He works now for the U.S. Air Force Futures office on the Information Warfare Capability Development Team. His work has previously appeared in the anthology Giant Robot Poems: On Mecha-Human Culture, Science & War *(Middle West Press, 2024), and in the Science Fiction & Fantasy Poetry Association's on-line journal* Eye to the Telescope.

Somewhere in Ohio
by Bella Rotker

hoophouses turn over dry dirt—men pull wheelbarrows weighed down with unsellable crops—unbearable ripeness—long days unearth themselves—I confront my girlhood by the radishes—the girl is beautiful—dust settles in slow motion—arms distance—I retreat—denim thick with dirt—a sparrow falls from the tree—above me—the moon hangs low like ripe fruit—I know the water will not run again—like I know this becoming unearthed—a siren rings through the night—I know how soil scars the skin—I know I am slowly becoming empty again—I dig up roots—eat a rutabaga rough with dirt—this bitterness like a girl's—what my mother gave me—she will not get back—everything painted orange in the evening—when I hold the girl we will be beautiful—orange feathers returning to dirt—how my mother wanted me to be beautiful—the girl finds my mouth as if homegrown—inimitable—she knows also that I am not—I was raised between corn rows—stalks stored tall in silos—above men's heads—we harvest in fall—are hungry again by winter

Bella Rotker is a proud Venezuelan and 305 local. A 5-time YoungArts winner and Best of The Net nominee, her work appears in Fifth Wheel Press, JAKE, *and elsewhere. When not writing or making shadow puppets, Rotker is thinking about cafecitos and bodies of water. "Somewhere in Ohio" previously appeared in* Eunoia Review. *Visit: bit.ly/bellarotker*

trip
by J. Chad Kebrdle

they all went on a trip that night
under constellations and moonlight
against the backdrop of forest and fire
dancing laughing in cleansing smoke
perfumes of pine and cedar
citronella and cannabis
pulsing against rhythms of music
the corn swaying against itself
and the universe
gathered in kindness and curiosity
chemically enhanced super-humans
swirling fractals
spinning blades of the windmills
towers watching over all
red eyes blinking on the dark horizon
"molock is here too"
says luke with his afro locks blowing down
licking at his flushed cheeks
paying no mind to frolicking satyrs
spinning out in a wooded clearing
within neatly lined field
care of monsanto and pioneer
on ground once considered unlivable
too hot in the summer
too cold in the winter
fertile soil now barren
stripped of riches and forests
casting echoes of history
against the overworked lands
once trodden upon by its natives
piankashaw and miami

dancing with us in the warm inky air
whispering for us to listen
and breathe

J. Chad Kebrdle holds an undergraduate degree in English from Ball State University, a graduate degree in liberal studies from Indiana University Kokomo, and a Master of Fine Arts in Creative Writing from the Jack Kerouac School of Disembodied Poetics at Naropa University, Boulder, Colorado. He has published work in journals including From the Wellhouse, A Common Thread, *and* Toasted Cheese. *He lives in an old farmhouse in a used-to-be town between two wanna-be cities, from which he draws his inspiration.*

Down on the Farm
By James Rumpel

As expected, Roger McConnell showed up at the Lane farm less than an hour after Dale's father's funeral. McConnell's black sports car skidded to a complete halt and its front doors lifted upward. To Dale, it looked like a hawk swooping in to grab its prey.

Roger McConnell was a charismatic man. You don't become the owner of the largest farm in Iowa without being able to get along with people. McConnell's 7,000-acre farm covered over 1000 square miles. There were two towns and a small city within its borders. Most of the residents of those boroughs worked for McConnell in one way or another.

"Hello, Dale," said McConnell, "I want to pay my respects to your father. I trust it was a nice service."

Dale nodded. "It was."

"I came to make a new offer. Your father didn't want to sell, but I'm sure he didn't want you chained down by this old out-of-date operation. I'm willing to pay you twice the last offer."

"I promised Dad I wouldn't sell."

"That's just not smart," said McConnell. "You can't make money. Your father sunk every cent he had, including your inheritance, into this place. It can't succeed. It's too small. It doesn't have AI machinery. You can't afford fast germinating seeds or mega-fertilizer. I bet you only get one crop per year. I get four and at a higher yield. This farm is a dinosaur."

Dale shrugged. "I'll think of something."

As the day's third tour bus, this one coming from out of state, pulled up the driveway, Dale took a deep breath. He looked at the run-down barn, slightly askew corn crib, and outdated solar tractor. It wasn't exactly what his father had hoped for, but the farm was surviving. Dale smiled. Dad would be proud.

James Rumpel is a retired high-school math teacher who enjoys spending some of his free time trying to turn a few of the odd ideas circling his brain into actual stories. He lives in Wisconsin with his wonderful wife, Mary.

When first the winds of change return home
by Brittany Redd

Seeds scattering solarpunk dreams—
a vision of sky; the night sky a beacon,
the day sky, too.
The soiled earth not recoiling, but making
something new
Green phoenix
Silver-glinted bullet train bonanza
And we become the sunflower, turning towards the sun
And also the moon
Tides rising, tides tempered;
annihilation overcome.
The blood and rot do make such fertile ground.

The New Garden of Eden; The Hanging Gardens of Babylon 2.0—
and here, the fruit is plentiful and
not forbidden

Prosperity promised, delivered.

Brittany Redd (she/they) is a teacher and writer currently based in Thailand. Her work appears or is forthcoming in Funicular Magazine, Quail Bell Magazine, Zehlreg A. Grindstone's Spectacular Western Oddity Emporium, *and elsewhere.*

Giving Years
by Jared Spears

Rough-hewn stoics,
men and women tired-eyed
in the pre-dawn, to take
in full advantage
the precious winter light
for their work, out on
some cold stretch of prairie,
miles from where two
roads used to meet.

Amid hammering jacks
and heaving steel barrows
this handful toil, bundled
under hard hats and gear:
breaking weathered asphalt,
fissuring the blacktop
every day until
the sun dips into
its long horizon.

The paved road grows
that much shorter, the
rubble spread a little further,
baring the earthy smell of soil
to the sweet air.

Every day is worth that:
hastening the reclamation.

Giving years.

Jared Spears is a writer who lives in in Hudson, New York. His work has appeared in Strukturriss, The Rumpus, Asymptote Journal, LitHub, *and elsewhere. He is originally from Pittsburg h, Pennsylvania.*

Discussion & Writing Prompts

Topic: "The Climes, They are A-Changin'"

Climate-change, unsurprisingly, is a concern of writers everywhere, including those describing and forecasting the American Midwest.

In "Arctic Winds in Wisconsin" (page 51), F. Malanoche starts "My mother always / Said there are no snow / Days in adulthood. // Thirty years later, / I huddle under / My cotton bed sheets. [...]"

In "White Stripes" (page 53), outdoor sports writer and poet Eric Chandler laments the loss of powder sufficient to support a lifetime of cross-country skiing: "like someone giving a demonstration of how to spin yarn / an activity that nobody does anymore // like going to a historic fort at a national park / where the reenactors line up and pretend to fight a historic battle // the old man will reenact the ancient gliding ritual across the / White stripe of manmade snow[.]"

Others address those in power, who have chosen to exploit people and resources rather than offer solutions. In the poem "Texas Innovation" (page 58), N. Jed Todd writes: "it occurs to me that out there, somewhere, alive this very day / Is the first guy to be convicted for insider trading / Against climate change. And you know it's a guy. / Some East Coast Ivy-League legacy in a suit / As expensive as the farmer's pickup truck / In whom he 'invests.'"

Writing Prompt:
Describe one or more ways that weather-trends are affecting your daily personal or professional life. Write a letter, an elegy, or some other form of prose or poetry, with the objective of sharing your experiences with someone who does not live or work near you, whether in space or time. It could be funny or sad, evocative or just-the-facts. What would you like them to know? What would you like them to feel?

Topic: "Losing Ourselves in Nature"

In newly written eco-mythologies, "going green" does not always result in positive outcomes for humankind. In "The Day the Trees Retaliate" (page 23), for example, poet Wendy BooydeGraaff writes about "trees who absorbed / human ways rather than the other / way 'round."

In "Invasive Species" (page 57), poet D.A. Gray writes, "[T]his stand of catclaw vine feasting on the fallen / then moving on, wrapping itself around, choking, / the living. It never seems to be an invasion / when you're hungry."

In "Underneath this surface" (page 38), one of three "Sporror" poems featured in this anthology, Mahaila Smith writes a voice who surrenders to "tendrils of the aggressive microfungi" that "weave new internal networks" in its victims. The poet-protagonist continues: "I had hoped to walk towards the next town / or the next. To find somewhere / the hyphae lost. / I condemn myself to solitude."

Writing Prompt:
Think about a time that you were surprised—perhaps scared, or awestruck—by encountering something "natural" in the world. Was it embodied by "flora" or "fauna"? (Or, if you prefer, "animal, vegetable, or mineral"?) Was it a personal experience, or a scientific epiphany? Write about that experience. Include plenty of sensory details. Now, consider anthropomorphizing your described item or idea—this time, writing from "Nature's" point-of-view.

Topic: "On Ruins, Nations, and Ruinations"

Even before Percy Bysshe Shelley (1792-1822) wrote "Ozymandias," poets have explored the meanings to be found in built and abandoned structures. Writers of the future American Midwest are no different.

In the poem "trip" (page 61), J. Chad Kerbdle's "chemically enhanced super-humans" acknowledge their connections: "fertile soil now barren / stripped of riches and forests / casting echoes of history / against the overworked lands / once trodden upon by its natives / piankashaw and miami / dancing with us in the warm inky air[.]"

In "Meet Me in Saint Louis (Lifecycle of a City)" (page 20), Benjamin B. White writes of a lost urban setting: "[...] In neighborhoods full / Of select Judy Garland mansions / Abandoned in a sad musical depiction / Of the blues floating by / Letting simplicity turn complex / With social attitudes and fear [...]"

James Rumpel's micro-fiction "Down on the Farm" (page 63) relates how a new generation survives by repurposing the tools and familial lands they now steward.

In "Giving Years" (page 66), poet Jared Spears describes releasing the land from its paved sarcophagus: "[...] Amid hammering jacks / and heaving steel barrows this handful toil, bundled under hard hats and gear: breaking weathered asphalt, fissuring the blacktop / every day until / the sun dips into / its long horizon. [...]"

Writing Prompt:
How do we change the land? How does the land change us? Write about something built on the land. Describe the object. How does the object change the use or interpretation of the space it occupies? What does it say about those who built or maintain it? How could it be repurposed? Should it be removed? Why?

Topic: "Fires, Floods, and Popcorn"

To quote Robert Frost's (1874-1963) poem "Fire and Ice": "Some say the world will end in fire, some say in ice." A number of contributors to this anthology creatively offered additional visions of apocalypse, including ash and flood.

In "Under Soft Rains" (page 42), for example, Zebulon Huset writes of a distant and unspecified disaster, which has manifested locally in orange sky and ash: "Once the snow fell and melted it washed away most of the ash. We grew some bumps, coughed more than we remembered, found more dead gulls than normal, but for the most part life rolled on."

In the prose-poem "When the mayor tells us to shower with a buddy" (page 22), Bethany Tap describes how rising waters untether us from feelings of safety and security: "[...] We'll be told to stay home, conserve water, and respect the river. Knee-deep in our wet former-lawns we will wander and wonder at the landscape transformed, at this brave new watery world, at the assumption we've always held: that we are the masters, that any of this is ours."

In Charlotte Brookins' "Midwestern Gold" (page 15), the storyteller offers a Jiffy Pop vision of fiery revelation: "As I flee town on asphalt that cleaves through the Heartland like a teaspoon through half-warmed margarine, passing wind turbines with red eyes that blink like they know what I did when I was fourteen under the summer Missouri sky, the familiar aroma of cow shit and stale air will be usurped by the popping of corn."

Writing Prompt:
Predict a world's end—or, perhaps, offer readers a choice of two. What environmental or human-made catastrophes can you forecast? What will end the Midwest (or another geographic region) to exist as we know it? Be cheeky about it. Or melancholy. Take your pick.

Topic: "Oh, Those Stoic Pioneers!"

Perhaps reflecting the assumed isolation of rural geographies, a recurring stereotype of Midwesterners is that they are both physically and emotionally isolated, accustomed to loneliness and harsh weather, and struggling for survival.

In "Giving Years" (page 66), for example, poet Jared Spears describes "Rough-hewn stoics, / men and women tired-eyed in the pre-dawn, to take / in full advantage the precious winter light / for their work, out on / some cold stretch of prairie, miles from where two roads used to meet."

In a possible post-apocalypse of Bella Rotker's "Rain Country" (page 3), the poet evokes the Midwestern hardworking spirit: "I am a servant / to this world of hurt. Always something undoing. Cicadas singing in the dark / of night. In the morning, we will rise / and return to our work. There are hides / to stretch and clean. Linens to rewash."

In "We'll Still Be Here" (page 34), poet Zackary Ross Wiggs shares a litany of future portends, including: "When the locusts / Finally fall silent ... // When dust chokes / The Midwest skies again ... // When the last . Dollar Store boards up ..."

Writing Prompt:
Brainstorm a list of ways we hide truths from one another, and ourselves. What are your "tells"—non-verbal behaviors that may reveal your inner feelings, decisions, or opinions? Write about a time you hid (or revealed) a truth, or faced a hard situation with a brave face.

Topic: "Wanted: A Few Good Neighbors"

In the 1957 script and music of 1957's "The Music Man," Iowan Meredith Wilson (1922-1984) captured a particular characteristic of Midwesterners, sometimes called "Iowa Nice." The stereotype is that people can seem polite, but are privately stand-offish and judgmental.

The lyrics to Wilson's song "Iowa Stubborn" include these lines: "We can be cold / As a falling thermometer in December / If you ask about our weather in July // And we're so by-God stubborn / We could stand touchin' noses / For a week at a time / And never see eye-to-eye [...]"

In "A Tale of Acceptable Loss" (page 9), D.A. Gray writes about the dangers of maintaining such unneighborly distances:

> "[...] We thrive together or We perish together.
>   The sign enraged the celebrants
> who shouted, Nature will not replace us!
>   Before the tear gas
> the cameras cut away and the station
>   brought in a scientist
> who speculated the cost of inaction
>   in terms of lives,
> while a politician across the desk
>   responded, Well, OK,
> long as it's someone else's child."

Writing Prompt:
Write about a time when you perceived, built, or removed a barrier that separated people. The obstacle could be physical, such as a wall or fence. Or it could be attitudinal, spiritual, or emotional. What factors created the opportunity for the change, for good or ill?

Topic: "Who We Are is Where We Have Been"

In "So Long, Lake of Stars" (page 5), Martin Ott reflects upon a star-filled Lake Huron, visible from a childhood window, and how the memory propelled him toward a new life.

In "Flight Attendants" (page 16), Herb Kauderer cheekily suggests that ethanol distilled from Iowa corn might one-day empower both humans and hogs to escape Earth's atmosphere with a "meat-and-potatoes practicality."

In Nayt Rundquist's haunting "SouLoans(tm)" (page 18), a character essentially reverse-mortgages a physical form, to transform toward new futures: "She steps aside, shrugs out of her body. As it slumps to the floor, she flutters off to find tech to hermit crab into and start anew."

Writing Prompt:
Write about leaving a familiar terrain, or choosing to stay. Perhaps you took some of that place with you, whether physically or metaphysically. What factors inspired your decision? What sense-memories, vocabulary, habits, or values of that place remain with you?

About the Editor

Randy "Sherpa" Brown traveled the world as a child in an active-duty U.S. Air Force family in the 1970s, then landed permanently and happily in the American Midwest. A former editor of community and metro newspapers, as well as national trade and "how-to" consumer magazines, he is now a freelance writer and editor based in Central Iowa.

Brown embedded with his former Iowa Army National Guard unit as a civilian journalist in Afghanistan, May-June 2011. A 20-year military veteran with one overseas deployment, he subsequently authored the award-winning 2015 collection *Welcome to FOB Haiku: War Poems from Inside the Wire*. More recently, he edited an anthology of speculative poetry, *Giant Robot Poems: Mecha-Human Science, Technology & War*.

His poetry and essays have appeared widely in print and on-line, as well as in anthologies. He notably appeared as himself in the soon-to-be-reissued 2021 *True War Stories* comic-book anthology.

Brown is a three-time poetry finalist in the Col. Darron L. Wright Memorial Writing Awards. He co-edited the 2019 Military Writers Guild anthology *Why We Write: Craft Essays on Writing War*, and the 2023 anthology *Things We Carry Still: Poems & Micro-Stories about Military Gear*. He also curated 2016's *Reporting for Duty: U.S. Citizen-Soldier Journalism from the Afghan Surge, 2010-2011*.

Brown was the winner of the 2018 "Untold Stories" poetry contest administered by *Flyover: Journal of Writing & the Environment*. He was the 2015 winner of the inaugural Madigan Award for humorous military-themed writing, presented by Negative Capability Press, Mobile, Alabama.

He is the current poetry editor at the literary journal *As You Were*, published twice a year by the non-profit Military Experience & the Arts. He is a member of the Military Writers Society of America (MWSA) and the Science Fiction and Fantasy Poetry Association (SFPA). He is a past board member of the Military Writers Guild and a past member of Military Reporters & Editors (MRE).

For more info, visit: linktr.ee/randysherpabrown

About Middle West Press

"Middle West Press LLC is a Johnston, Iowa-based editor and publisher of non-fiction, fiction, journalism, and poetry. As an independent micro-press, we publish from one to four titles annually. Our projects are often inspired by the people, places, and history of the American Midwest."

In its publishing operations, Middle West Press LLC specializes in book-length projects, such as themed literary and non-fiction anthologies, as well as single-author poetry collections. In terms of business models, we are a traditional press. "We pay our authors; they do not pay us."

As a secondary mission—beyond the American Midwest—we are also motivated to illuminate and complicate modern stereotypes related to military service and veterancy. We want to challenge readers to move beyond Hollywood's "American Snipers and Navy SEALs" and "TYFYS." We also believe that "Everyone has an experience with the military, even if only as taxpayer and voter."

More generally, we are interested in celebrating and featuring voices such as those of women, writers of color, writers who identify as LGBTQ+, and other historically marginalized populations.

We publish from 1 to 4 titles annually. At least one of these is usually a collection of poetry, and one is a themed anthology.

We use Publish-on-Demand (POD) technology to print our physical editions. This means that a copy of any given book title is printed only at the time of purchase. Our aim is to avoid cluttering warehouses and authors' basements with unsold or dusty overstock.

Finally, in both practice and principle, we subscribe to the objectives of clarity, transparency, and literary citizenship as described in the Community of Literary Magazines & Presses' code of ethics.

Anthologies
Published by Middle West Press

Giant Robot Poems:
On Mecha-Human Science, Culture & War
Edited by Randy Brown

Our Best War Stories:
Prize-winning Poetry & Prose
from the Col. Darron L. Wright Memorial Awards
Edited by Christopher Lyke

Why We Write:
Craft Essays on Writing War
Edited by Steve Leonard and Randy Brown

Things We Carry Still:
Poems & Micro-Stories about Military Gear
Edited by Lisa Stice and Randy Brown

Forthcoming in 2025!

Cryptids, Kaiju & Corn:
Poems and Micro-Stories about Modern Midwest Monsters
Edited by Randy Brown

Single-Author Collections Published by Middle West Press

Hugging This Rock: Poems of Earth & Sky, Love & War
by Eric Chandler

Permanent Change of Station, FORCES,
and *Letters from Conflict*
by Lisa Stice

The Explosion Takes Both Legs: Noir Poems from the War in Iraq
by J.B. Stevens

Paying for Gas with Quarters: A Parent's Odyssey in Poems
by Aly Allen

Always Ready: Poems from a Life in the U.S. Coast Guard
by Benjamin B. White

The Time War Takes
by Jessi M. Atherton

Unwound: Poems from Enduring Wars
by Liam Corley

September Eleventh: an epic poem, in fragments
by Amalie Flynn

HEAT + PRESSURE: Poems from War
by Ben Weakley

Blood / Not Blood, Then the Gates
by Ron Riekki

Did You Enjoy This Book?

Tell your friends and family about it! Post your thoughts via social media sites, like Facebook, Instagram, Threads, Twitter/X, and Bluesky!

You can also share a quick review on websites for other readers, such as Goodreads.com! Or offer your impressions on bookseller websites, such as Amazon.com and BarnesandNoble.com!

Recommend the title to your favorite local library, book club, or independent bookstore!

Remember, there is nothing more powerful in business of publishing than a shared rating, review, or recommendation from a friend. We appreciate your support!

You can find us at:

Middle West Press LLC
P.O. Box 1153
Johnston, Iowa 50131-9420

Or visit: **www.middlewestpress.com**

www.ingramcontent.com/pod-product-compliance
Lightning Source LLC
Chambersburg PA
CBHW051932240626
47153CB00004B/1455